Main Street

Nathaniel Hawthorne

Main Street

Respectable-looking individual makes his bow and addresses the public. In my daily walks along the principal street of my native town, it has often occurred to me, that, if its growth from infancy upward, and the vicissitude of characteristic scenes that have passed along this thoroughfare during the more than two centuries of its existence, could be presented to the eye in a shifting panorama, it would bean exceedingly effective method of illustrating the march of time. Acting on this idea, I have contrived a certain pictorial exhibition, somewhat in the nature of a puppet-show, by means of which I propose to call up the multiform and many-colored Past before the spectator, and show him the ghosts of his forefathers, amid a succession of historic incidents, with no greater trouble than the turning of a crank. Be pleased, therefore, my indulgent patrons, to walk into the show-room, and take your seats before yonder mysterious curtain. The little wheels and springs of my machinery have been well oiled; a multitude of puppets are dressed in character, representing all varieties of fashion, from the Puritan cloak and jerkin to the latest Oak Hall coat; the lamps are trimmed, and shall brighten into noontide sunshine, or fade away in moonlight, or muffle their brilliancy in a November cloud, as the nature of the scene may require; and, in short, the exhibition is just ready to commence. Unless something should go wrong,— as, for instance, the misplacing of a picture, whereby the people and events of one century might be thrust into the middle of another; or the breaking of a wire, which would bring the course of time to a sudden period,—barring, I say, the casualties to which such a complicated piece of mechanism is liable, —I flatter myself, ladies and gentlemen,—that the performance will elicit your generous approbation.

Ting-a-ting-ting! goes the bell; the curtain rises; and we behold-not, indeed, the Main Street—but the track of leaf-strewn forest-land over which its dusty pavement is hereafter to extend.

You perceive, at a glance, that this is the ancient and primitive wood,—the ever-youthful and venerably old,—verdant with new twigs, yet hoary, as it were, with the snowfall of innumerable years, that have accumulated upon its intermingled branches. The white man's axe has never smitten a single tree; his footstep has never crumpled a single one of the withered leaves, which all the autumns since the flood have been harvesting beneath. Yet, see! along through the vista of impending boughs, there is already a faintly traced path, running nearly east and west, as if a prophecy or foreboding of the future street had stolen into the heart of the solemn old wood. Onward goes this hardly perceptible track, now ascending over a natural swell of land, now subsiding gently into a hollow; traversed here by a little streamlet, which glitters like a snake through the gleam of sunshine, and quickly hides itself among the underbrush, in its quest for the neighboring cove; and impeded there by the massy corpse of a giant of the forest, which had lived out its incalculable term of life, and been overthrown by mere old age, and lies buried in the new vegetation that is born of its decay. What footsteps can have worn this half-seen path? Hark! Do we not hear them now rustling softly over the leaves? We discern an Indian woman,—a majestic and queenly woman, or else her spectral image does not represent her truly,—for this is the great Squaw Sachem, whose rule, with that of her sons, extends from Mystic to Agawam. That red chief, who stalks by her side, is Wappacowet, her second husband, the priest and magician, whose incantations shall hereafter affright the pale-faced settlers with grisly phantoms, dancing and shrieking in the woods, at midnight. But greater would be the affright of the Indian necromancer, if, mirrored in the pool of water at his feet, he could catch a prophetic glimpse of the noonday marvels which the white man is destined to achieve; if he could see, as in a dream, the stone front of the stately hall, which will cast its shadow over this very spot; if he could be aware that the future edifice will contain a noble Museum, where, among countless curiosities of earth and sea, a few Indian arrow-heads shall be treasured up as memorials of a vanished race!

No such forebodings disturb the Squaw Sachem and Wappacowet. They pass on, beneath the tangled shade, holding high talk on matters of state and religion, and imagine, doubtless, that their own system of affairs will endure forever. Meanwhile, how full of its own proper life is the scene that lies around them! The gray squirrel runs up the trees, and rustles among the upper branches. Was not that the leap of a deer? And there is the whirr of a partridge! Methinks, too, I catch the cruel and stealthy eye of a wolf, as he draws back into yonder impervious density of underbrush. So, there, amid the murmur of boughs, go the Indian queen and the Indian priest; while the gloom of the broad wilderness impends over them, and its sombre mystery invests them as with something preternatural; and only momentary streaks of quivering sunlight, once in a great while, find their way down, and glimmer among the feathers in their dusky hair. Can it be that the thronged street of a city will ever pass into this twilight solitude,—over those soft heaps of the decaying tree-trunks, and through the swampy places, green with water-moss, and penetrate that hopeless entanglement of great trees, which have been uprooted and tossed together by a whirlwind? It has been a wilderness from the creation. Must it not be a wilderness forever?

Here an acidulous-looking gentleman in blue glasses, with bows of Berlin steel, who has taken a seat at the extremity of the front row, begins, at this early stage of the exhibition, to criticise.

"The whole affair is a manifest catchpenny!" observes he, scarcely under his breath. "The trees look more like weeds in a garden than a primitive forest; the Squaw Sachem and Wappacowet are stiff in their pasteboard joints; and the squirrels, the deer, and the wolf move with all the grace of a child's wooden monkey, sliding up and down a stick."

"I am obliged to you, sir, for the candor of your remarks," replies the showman, with a bow. "Perhaps they are just. Human art has its limits, and we must now and then ask a little aid from the spectator's imagination."

"You will get no such aid from mine," responds the critic. "I make it a point to see things precisely as they are. But come! go ahead! the stage is waiting!"

The showman proceeds.

Casting our eyes again over the scene, we perceive that strangers have found their way into the solitary place. In more than one spot, among the trees, an upheaved axe is glittering in the sunshine. Roger Conant, the first settler in Naumkeag, has built his dwelling, months ago, on the border of the forest-path; and at this moment he comes eastward through the vista of woods, with his gun over his shoulder, bringing home the choice portions of a deer. His stalwart figure, clad in a leathern jerkin and breeches of the same, strides sturdily onward, with such an air of physical force and energy that we might almost expect the very trees to stand aside, and give him room to pass. And so, indeed, they must; for, humble as is his name in history, Roger Conant still is of that class of men who do not merely find, but make, their place in the system of human affairs; a man of thoughtful strength, he has planted the germ of a city. There stands his habitation, showing in its rough architecture some features of the Indian wigwam, and some of the log-cabin, and somewhat, too, of the straw-thatched cottage in Old England, where this good yeoman had his birth and breeding. The dwelling is surrounded by a cleared space of a few acres, where Indian corn grows thrivingly among the stumps of the trees; while the dark forest hems it in, and scenes to gaze silently and solemnly, as if wondering at the breadth of sunshine which the white man spreads around him. An Indian, half hidden in the dusky shade, is gazing and wondering too.

Within the door of the cottage you discern the wife, with her ruddy English cheek. She is singing, doubtless, a psalm tune, at her household work; or, perhaps she sighs at the remembrance of the cheerful gossip, and all the merry social life, of her native village beyond the vast and melancholy sea. Yet the next moment she laughs, with sympathetic glee, at the sports of her little tribe of children; and soon turns round, with the home-look in her face, as her husband's foot is heard approaching the rough-hewn threshold. How sweet must it be for those who have an Eden in their hearts, like Roger Conant and his wife, to find a new world to project it into, as they have, instead of dwelling among old haunts of men, where so many household fires have been kindled and burnt out, that the very glow of happiness has something dreary in it! Not that this pair are alone in their wild Eden, for here comes Goodwife Massey, the young spouse of Jeffrey Massey, from her home hard by, with an infant at her breast. Dame Conant has another of like age; and it shall hereafter be one of the disputed points of history which of these two babies was the first town-born child.

But see! Roger Conant has other neighbors within view. Peter Palfrey likewise has built himself a house, and so has Balch, and Norman, and Woodbury. Their dwellings, indeed,—such is the ingenious contrivance of this piece of pictorial mechanism,—seem to have arisen, at various points of the scene, even while we have been looking at it. The forest-track, trodden more and more by the hobnailed shoes of these sturdy and ponderous Englishmen, has now a distinctness which it never could have acquired from the light tread of a hundred times as many Indian moccasins. It will be a street, anon! As we observe it now, it goes onward from one clearing to another, here plunging into a shadowy strip of woods, there open to the sunshine, but everywhere showing a decided line, along which human interests have begun to hold their career. Over yonder swampy spot, two trees have been felled, and laid side by side to make a causeway. In another place, the axe has cleared away a confused intricacy of fallen trees and clustered boughs, which had been tossed together by a hurricane. So now the little children, just beginning to run alone, may trip along the path, and not often stumble over an impediment, unless they stray from it to gather wood-berries beneath the trees. And, besides the feet of grown people and children, there are the cloven hoofs of a small herd of cows, who seek their subsistence from the native grasses, and help to deepen the track of the future thoroughfare. Goats also browse along it, and nibble at the twigs that thrust themselves across the way. Not seldom, in its more secluded portions, where the black shadow of the forest strives to hide the trace of human-footsteps, stalks a gaunt wolf, on the watch for a kid or a young calf; or fixes his hungry gaze on the group of children gathering berries, and can hardly forbear to rush upon them. And the Indians, coming from their distant wigwams to view the white man's settlement, marvel at the deep track which he makes, and perhaps are saddened by a flitting presentiment that this heavy tread will find its way over all the land; and that the wild-woods, the wild wolf, and the wild Indian will alike be trampled beneath it. Even so shall it be. The pavements of the Main Street must be laid over the red man's grave.

Behold! here is a spectacle which should be ushered in by the peal of trumpets, if Naumkeag had ever yet heard that cheery music, and by the roar of cannon, echoing among the woods. A procession,—for, by its dignity, as marking an epoch in the history of the street, it deserves that name,—a procession advances along the pathway. The good ship Abigail has arrived from England, bringing wares and merchandise, for the comfort of the inhabitants, and traffic with the Indians; bringing passengers too, and, more important than all, a governor for the new settlement. Roger Conant and Peter Palfrey, with their companions, have been to the shore to welcome him; and now, with such honor and triumph as their rude way of life permits, are escorting the sea-flushed voyagers to their habitations. At the point where Endicott enters upon the scene, two venerable trees unite their branches high above his head; thus forming a triumphal arch of living verdure, beneath which he pauses, with his wife leaning on his arm, to catch the first impression of their new-found home. The old settlers gaze not less earnestly at him, than he at the hoary woods and the rough surface of the clearings. They like his bearded face, under the shadow of the broad-brimmed and steeple-crowned Puritan hat;—a visage resolute, grave, and thoughtful, yet apt to kindle with that glow of a cheerful spirit by which men of strong character are enabled to go joyfully on their proper tasks. His form, too, as you see it, in a doublet and hose of sad-colored cloth, is of a manly make, fit for toil and hardship, and fit to wield the heavy sword that hangs from his leathern belt. His aspect is a better warrant for the ruler's office than the parchment commission which he bears, however fortified it may be with the broad seal of the London council.

Peter Palfrey nods to Roger Conant. "The worshipful Court of Assistants have done wisely," say they between themselves. "They have chosen for our governor a man out of a thousand." Then they toss up their hats,—they, and all the uncouth figures of their company, most of whom are clad in skins, inasmuch as their old kersey and linsey-woolsey garments have been torn and tattered by many a long month's wear,—they all toss up their hats, and salute their new governor and captain with a hearty English shout of welcome. We seem to hear it with our own ears, so perfectly is the action represented in this life-like, this almost magic picture! But have you observed the lady who leans upon the arm of Endicott?——a rose of beauty from an English garden, now to be transplanted to a fresher soil. It may be that, long years—centuries indeed —after this fair flower shall have decayed, other flowers of the same race will appear in the same soil, and gladden other generations with hereditary beauty. Does not the vision haunt us yet? Has not Nature kept the mould unbroken, deeming it a pity that the idea should vanish from mortal sight forever, after only once assuming earthly substance? Do we not recognize, in that fair woman's face, a model of features which still beam, at happy meets, on what was then the woodland pathway, but has out since grown into a busy street?

"This is too ridiculous!—positively insufferable!" mutters the same critic who had before expressed his disapprobation. "Here is a pasteboard figure, such as a child would cut out of a card, with a pair of very dull scissors; and the fellow modestly requests us to see in it the prototype of hereditary beauty!"

"But, sir, you have not the proper point of view," remarks the showman. "You sit altogether too near to get the best effect of my pictorial exhibition. Pray, oblige me by removing to this other bench, and I venture assure you the proper light and shadow will transform the spectacle into quite another thing."

"Pshaw!" replies the critic; "I want no other light and shade. I have already told you that it is my business to see things just as they are."

"I would suggest to the author of this ingenious exhibition," observes a gentlemanly person, who has shown signs of being much interested,—"I would suggest that Anna Gower, the first wife of Governor Endicott, and who came with him from England, left no posterity; and that, consequently, we cannot be indebted to that honorable lady for any specimens of feminine loveliness now extant among us."

Having nothing to allege against this genealogical objection, the showman points again to the scene.

During this little interruption, you perceive that the Anglo-Saxon energy—as the phrase now goes—has been at work in the spectacle before us. So many chimneys now send up their smoke, that it begins to have the aspect of a village street; although everything is so inartificial and inceptive, that it seems as if one returning wave of the wild nature might overwhelm it all. But the one edifice which gives the pledge of permanence to this bold enterprise is seen at the central point of the picture. There stands the meeting-house, a small structure, low-roofed, without a spire, and built of rough timber, newly hewn, with the sap still in the logs, and here and there a strip of bark adhering to them. A meaner temple was never consecrated to the worship of the Deity. With the alternative of kneeling beneath the awful vault of the firmament, it is strange that men should creep into this pent-up nook, and expect God's presence there. Such, at least, one would imagine, might be the feeling of these forest-settlers, accustomed, as they had been, to stand under the dim arches of vast cathedrals, and to offer up their hereditary worship in the old ivy-covered churches of rural England, around which lay the bones of many generations of their forefathers. How could they dispense with the carved altar-work?—how, with the pictured windows, where the light of common day was hallowed by being transmitted through the glorified figures of saints?— how, with the lofty roof, imbued, as it must have been, with the prayers that had gone upward for centuries?—how, with the rich peal of the solemn organ, rolling along the aisles, pervading the whole church, and sweeping the soul away on a flood of audible religion? They needed nothing of all this. Their house of worship, like their ceremonial, was naked, simple, and severe. But the zeal of a recovered faith burned like a lamp within their hearts, enriching everything around them with its radiance; making of these new walls, and this narrow compass, its own cathedral; and being, in itself, that spiritual mystery and experience, of which sacred architecture, pictured windows, and the organ's grand solemnity are remote and imperfect symbols. All was well, so long as their lamps were freshly kindled at heavenly flame. After a while, however, whether in their time or their children's, these lamps began to burn more dimly, or with a less genuine lustre; and then it might be seen how hard, cold, and confined was their system,—how like an iron cage was that which they called Liberty.

Too much of this. Look again at the picture, and observe how the aforesaid Anglo-Saxon energy is now trampling along the street, and raising a positive cloud of dust beneath its sturdy footsteps. For there the carpenters are building a new house, the frame of which was hewn and fitted in England, of English oak, and sent hither on shipboard; and here a blacksmith makes huge slang and clatter on his anvil, shaping out tools and weapons; and yonder a wheelwright, who boasts himself a London workman, regularly bred to his handicraft, is fashioning a set of wagon-wheels, the track of which Wall soon be visible. The wild forest is shrinking back; the street has lost the aromatic odor of the pine-trees, and of the sweet-fern that grew beneath them. The tender and modest wild-flowers, those gentle children of savage nature that grew pale beneath the ever-brooding shade, have shrank away and disappeared, like stars that vanish in the breadth of light. Gardens are fenced in, and display pumpkin-beds and rows of cabbages and beans; and, though the governor and the minister both view them with a disapproving eye, plants of broad-leaved tobacco, which the cultivators are enjoined to use privily, or not at all. No wolf, for a year past, has been heard to bark, or known to range among the dwellings, except that single one, whose grisly head, with a plash of blood beneath it, is now affixed to the portal of the meeting-house. The partridge has ceased to run across the too-frequented path. Of all the wild life that used to throng here, only the Indians still come into the settlement, bringing the skins of beaver and otter, bear and elk, which they sell to Endicott for the wares of England. And there is little John Massey, the son of Jeffrey Massey and first-born of Naumkeag, playing beside his father's threshold, a child of six or seven years old. Which is the better-grown infant,—the town or the boy?

The red men have become aware that the street is no longer free to them, save by the sufferance and permission of the settlers. Often, to impress them with an awe of English power, there is a muster and training of the town-forces, and a stately march of the mail-clad band, like this which we now see advancing up the street. There they come, fifty of them, or more; all with their iron breastplates and steel caps well burnished, and glimmering bravely against the sun; their ponderous muskets on their shoulders, their bandaliers about their waists, their lighted matches in their hands, and the drum and fife playing cheerily before them. See! do they not step like martial men? Do they not manoeuvre like soldiers who have seen stricken fields? And well they may; for this band is composed of precisely such materials as those with which Cromwell is preparing to beat down the strength of a kingdom; and his famous regiment of Ironsides might be recruited from just such men. In everything, at this period, New England was the essential spirit and flower of that which was about to become uppermost in the mother-country. Many a bold and wise man lost the fame which would have accrued to him in English history, by crossing the Atlantic with our forefathers. Many a valiant captain, who might have been foremost at Marston Moor or Naseby, exhausted his martial ardor in the command of a log-built fortress, like that which you observe on the gently rising ground at the right of the pathway,—its banner fluttering in the breeze, and the culverins and sakers showing their deadly muzzles over the rampart.

A multitude of people were now thronging to New England: some, because the ancient and ponderous framework of Church and State threatened to crumble down upon their heads; others, because they despaired of such a downfall. Among those who came to Naumkeag were men of history and legend, whose feet leave a track of brightness along any pathway which they have trodden. You shall behold their life-like images—their spectres, if you choose so to call them—passing, encountering with a familiar nod, stopping to converse together, praying, bearing weapons, laboring or resting from their labors, in the Main Street. Here, now, comes Hugh Peters, an earnest, restless man, walking swiftly, as being impelled by that fiery activity of nature which shall hereafter thrust him into the conflict of dangerous affairs, make him the chaplain and counsellor of Cromwell, and finally bring him to a bloody end. He pauses, by the meetinghouse, to exchange a greeting with Roger Williams, whose face indicates, methinks, a gentler spirit, kinder and more expansive, than that of Peters; yet not less active for what he discerns to be the will of God, or the welfare of mankind. And look! here is a guest for Endicott, coming forth out of the forest, through which he has been journeying from Boston, and which, with its rude branches, has caught hold of his attire, and has wet his feet with its swamps and streams. Still there is something in his mild and venerable, though not aged presence—a propriety, an equilibrium, in Governor Winthrop's nature—that causes the disarray of his costume to be unnoticed, and gives us the same impression as if he were clad in such rave and rich attire as we may suppose him to have worn in the Council Chamber of the colony. Is not this characteristic wonderfully perceptible in our spectral representative of his person? But what dignitary is this crossing from the other side to greet the governor? A stately personage, in a dark velvet cloak, with a hoary beard, and a gold chain across his breast; he has the authoritative port of one who has filled the highest civic station in the first of cities. Of all men in the world, we should least expect to meet the Lord Mayor of London—as Sir Richard Saltonstall has been, once and again—in a forest-bordered settlement of the western wilderness.

Farther down the street, we see Emanuel Downing, a grave and worthy citizen, with his son George, a stripling who has a career before him; his shrewd and quick capacity and pliant conscience shall not only exalt him high, but secure him from a downfall. Here is another figure, on whose characteristic make and expressive action I will stake the credit of my pictorial puppet-show.

Have you not already detected a quaint, sly humor in that face,—an eccentricity in the manner,—a certain indescribable waywardness,—all the marks, in short, of an original man, unmistakably impressed, yet kept down by a sense of clerical restraint? That is Nathaniel Ward, the minister of Ipswich, but better remembered as the simple cobbler of Agawam. He hammered his sole so faithfully, and stitched his upper-leather so well, that the shoe is hardly yet worn out, though thrown aside for some two centuries past. And next, among these Puritans and Roundheads, we observe the very model of a Cavalier, with the curling lovelock, the fantastically trimmed beard, the embroidery, the ornamented rapier, the gilded dagger, and all other foppishnesses that distinguished the wild gallants who rode headlong to their overthrow in the cause of King Charles. This is Morton of Merry Mount, who has come hither to hold a council with Endicott, but will shortly be his prisoner. Yonder pale, decaying figure of a white-robed woman, who glides slowly along the street, is the Lady Arabella, looking for her own grave in the virgin soil. That other female form, who seems to be talking—we might almost say preaching or expounding—in the centre of a group of profoundly attentive auditors, is Ann Hutchinson. And here comes Vane—

"But, my dear sir," interrupts the same gentleman who before questioned the showman's genealogical accuracy, "allow me to observe that these historical personages could not possibly have met together in the Main Street. They might, and probably did, all visit our old town, at one time or another, but not simultaneously; and you have fallen into anachronisms that I positively shudder to think of!"

"The fellow," adds the scarcely civil critic, "has learned a bead-roll of historic names, whom he lugs into his pictorial puppet-show, as he calls it, helter-skelter, without caring whether they were contemporaries or not,—and sets them all by the ears together. But was there ever such a fund of impudence? To hear his running commentary, you would suppose that these miserable slips of painted pasteboard, with hardly the remotest outlines of the human figure, had all the character and expression of Michael Angele's pictures. Well! go on, sir!"

"Sir, you break the illusion of the scene," mildly remonstrates the showman.

"Illusion! What illusion?" rejoins the critic, with a contemptuous snort. "On the word of a gentleman, I see nothing illusive in the wretchedly bedaubed sheet of canvas that forms your background, or in these pasteboard slips that hitch and jerk along the front. The only illusion, permit me to say, is in the puppet-showman's tongue,—and that but a wretched one, into the bargain!"

"We public men," replies the showman, meekly, "must lay our account, sometimes, to meet an uncandid severity of criticism. But—merely for your own pleasure, sir—let me entreat you to take another point of view. Sit farther back, by that young lady, in whose face I have watched the reflection of every changing scene; only oblige me by sitting there; and, take my word for it, the slips of pasteboard shall assume spiritual life, and the bedaubed canvas become an airy and changeable reflex of what it purports to represent."

"I know better," retorts the critic, settling himself in his seat, with sullen but self-complacent immovableness. "And, as for my own pleasure, I shall best consult it by remaining precisely where I am."

The showman bows, and waves his hand; and, at the signal, as if time and vicissitude had been awaiting his permission to move onward, the mimic street becomes alive again.

Years have rolled over our scene, and converted the forest-track into a dusty thoroughfare, which, being intersected with lanes and cross-paths, may fairly be designated as the Main Street. On the ground-sites of many of the log-built sheds, into which the first settlers crept for shelter, houses of quaint architecture have now risen. These later edifices are built, as you see, in one generally accordant style, though with such subordinate variety as keeps the beholder's curiosity excited, and causes each structure, like its owner's character, to produce its own peculiar impression. Most of them have a huge chimney in the centre, with flues so vast that it must have been easy for the witches to fly out of them as they were wont to do, when bound on an aerial visit to the Black Man in the forest. Around this great chimney the wooden house clusters itself, in a whole community of gable-ends, each ascending into its own karate peak; the second story, with its lattice-windows, projecting over the first; and the door, which is perhaps arched, provided on the outside with an iron hammer, wherewith the visitor's hand may give a thundering rat-a-tat.

The timber framework of these houses, as compared with those of recent date, is like the skeleton of an old giant, beside the frail bones of a modern man of fashion. Many of them, by the vast strength and soundness of their oaken substance, have been preserved through a length of time which would have tried the stability of brick and stone; so that, in all the progressive decay and continual reconstruction of the street, down our own days, we shall still behold these old edifices occupying their long-accustomed sites. For instance, on the upper corner of that green lane which shall hereafter be North Street, we see the Curwen House, newly built, with the carpenters still at work on the roof nailing down the last sheaf of shingles. On the lower corner stands another dwelling,—destined, at some period of its existence, to be the abode of an unsuccessful alchemist,—which shall likewise survive to our own generation, and perhaps long outlive it. Thus, through the medium of these patriarchal edifices, we have now established a sort of kindred and hereditary acquaintance with the Main Street.

Great as is the transformation produced by a short term of years, each single day creeps through the Puritan settlement sluggishly enough. It shall pass before your eyes, condensed into the space of a few moments. The gray light of early morning is slowly diffusing itself over the scene; and the bellman, whose office it is to cry the hour at the street-corners, rings the last peal upon his hand bell, and goes wearily homewards, with the owls, the bats, and other creatures of the night. Lattices are thrust back on their hinges, as if the town were opening its eyes, in the summer morning. Forth stumbles the still drowsy cowherd, with his horn; putting which to his lips, it emits a bellowing bray, impossible to be represented in the picture, but which reaches the pricked-up ears of every cow in the settlement, and tells her that the dewy pasture-hour is come. House after house awakes, and sends the smoke up curling from its chimney, like frosty breath from living nostrils; and as those white wreaths of smoke, though impregnated with earthy admixtures, climb skyward, so, from each dwelling, does the morning worship—its spiritual essence, bearing up its human imperfection—find its way to the heavenly Father's throne.

The breakfast-hour being passed, the inhabitants do not, as usual, go to their fields or workshops, but remain within doors; or perhaps walk the street, with a grave sobriety, yet a disengaged and unburdened aspect, that belongs neither to a holiday nor a Sabbath. And, indeed, this passing day is neither, nor is it a common week-day, although partaking of all the three. It is the Thursday Lecture; an institution which New England has long ago relinquished, and almost forgotten, yet which it would have been better to retain, as bearing relations to both the spiritual and ordinary life, and bringing each acquainted with the other. The tokens of its observance, however, which here meet our eyes, are of rather a questionable cast. It is, in one sense, a day of public shame; the day on which transgressors, who have made themselves liable to the minor severities of the Puritan law receive their reward of ignominy. At this very moment, this constable has bound an idle fellow to the whipping-post, and is giving him his deserts with a cat-o'-nine tails. Ever since sunrise, Daniel Fairfield has been standing on the steps of the meeting-house, with a halter about his neck, which he is condemned to wear visibly throughout his lifetime; Dorothy Talby is chained to a post at the corner of Prison Lane, with the hot sun blazing on her matronly face, and all for no other offence than lifting her hand against her husband; while, through the bars of that great wooden cage, in the centre of the scene, we discern either a human being or a wild beast, or both in one, whom this public infamy causes to roar, and gnash his teeth, and shake the strong oaken bars, as if he would breakforth, and tear in pieces the little children who have been peeping at him. Such are the profitable sights that serve the good people to while away the earlier part of lecture-day. Betimes in the forenoon, a traveller—the first traveller that has come hitherward this morning-rides slowly into the street on his patient steed. He seems a clergyman; and, as he draws near, we recognize the minister of Lynn, who was pre-engaged to lecture here, and has been revolving his discourse, as he rode through the hoary wilderness. Behold, now, the whole town thronging into the meeting-house, mostly with such sombre visages that the sunshine becomes little better than a shadow when it falls upon them. There go the Thirteen Men, grim rulers of a grim community! There goes John Massey, the first town-born child, now a youth of twenty, whose eye wanders with peculiar interest towards that buxom damsel who comes up the steps at the same instant. There hobbles Goody Foster, a sour and bitter old beldam, looking as if she went to curse, and not to pray, and whom many of her neighbors suspect of taking an occasional airing on a broomstick. There, too, slinking shamefacedly in, you observe that same poor do-nothing and good-for-nothing whom we saw castigated just now at the whipping-post. Last of all, there goes the tithing-man, lugging in a couple of small boys, whom he has caught at play beneath God's blessed sunshine, in a back lane. What native of

Naumkeag, whose recollections go back more than thirty years, does not still shudder at that dark ogre of his infancy, who perhaps had long ceased to have an actual existence, but still lived in his childish belief, in a horrible idea, and in the nurse's threat, as the Tidy Man!

It will be hardly worth our while to wait two, or it may be three, turnings of the hour-glass, for the conclusion of the lecture. Therefore, by my control over light and darkness, I cause the dusk, and then the starless night, to brood over the street; and summon forth again the bellman, with his lantern casting a gleam about his footsteps, to pace wearily from corner to corner, and shout drowsily the hour to drowsy or dreaming ears. Happy are we, if for nothing else, yet because we did not live in those days. In truth, when the first novelty and stir of spirit had subsided,—when the new settlement, between the forest-border and the sea, had become actually a little town,—its daily life must have trudged onward with hardly anything to diversify and enliven it, while also its rigidity could not fail to cause miserable distortions of the moral nature. Such a life was sinister to the intellect, and sinister to the heart; especially when one generation had bequeathed its religious gloom, and the counterfeit of its religious ardor, to the next; for these characteristics, as was inevitable, assumed the form both of hypocrisy and exaggeration, by being inherited from the example and precept of other human beings, and not from an original and spiritual source. The sons and grandchildren of the first settlers were a race of lower and narrower souls than their progenitors had been. The latter were stern, severe, intolerant, but not superstitious, not even fanatical; and endowed, if any men of that age were, with a far-seeing worldly sagacity. But it was impossible for the succeeding race to grow up, in heaven's freedom, beneath the discipline which their gloomy energy of character had established; nor, it may be, have we even yet thrown off all the unfavorable influences which, among many good ones, were bequeathed to us by our Puritan forefathers. Let us thank God for having given us such ancestors; and let each successive generation thank him, not less fervently, for being one step further from them in the march of ages.

"What is all this?" cries the critic. "A sermon? If so, it is not in the bill."

"Very true," replies the showman; "and I ask pardon of the audience."

Look now at the street, and observe a strange people entering it. Their garments are torn and disordered, their faces haggard, their figures emaciated; for they have made their way hither through pathless deserts, suffering hunger and hardship, with no other shelter thin a hollow tree, the lair of a wild beast, or an Indian wigwam. Nor, in the most inhospitable and dangerous of such lodging-places, was there half the peril that awaits them in this thoroughfare of Christian men, with those secure dwellings and warm hearths on either side of it, and yonder meeting-house as the central object of the scene. These wanderers have received from Heaven a gift that, in all epochs of the world, has brought with it the penalties of mortal suffering and persecution, scorn, enmity, and death itself;—a gift that, thus terrible to its possessors, has ever been most hateful to all other men, since its very existence seems to threaten the overthrow of whatever else the toilsome ages have built up;—the gift of a new idea. You can discern it in them, illuminating their faces—their whole persons, indeed, however earthly and cloddish—with a light that inevitably shines through, and makes the startled community aware that these men are not as they themselves are,—not brethren nor neighbors of their thought. Forthwith, it is as if an earthquake rumbled through the town, making its vibrations felt at every hearthstone, and especially causing the spire of the meeting-house to totter. The Quakers have come. We are in peril! See! they trample upon our wise and well-established laws in the person of our chief magistrate; for Governor Endicott is passing, now an aged man, and dignified with long habits of authority,—and not one of the irreverent vagabonds has moved his bat. Did you note the ominous frown of the white-bearded Puritan governor, as he turned himself about, and, in his anger, half uplifted the staff that has become a needful support to his old age? Here comes old Mr. Norris, our venerable minister. Will they doff their hats, and pay reverence to him? No: their hats stick fast to their ungracious heads, as if they grew there; and— impious varlets that they are, and worse than the heathen Indians!—they eye our reverend pastor with a peculiar scorn, distrust, unbelief, and utter denial of his sanctified pretensions, of which he himself immediately becomes conscious; the more bitterly conscious, as he never knew nor dreamed of the like before.

But look yonder! Can we believe our eyes? A Quaker woman, clad in sackcloth, and with ashes on her head, has mounted the steps of the meeting-house. She addresses the people in a wild, shrill voice,—wild and shrill it must be to suit such a figure,—which makes them tremble and turn pale, although they crowd open-mouthed to hear her. She is bold against established authority; she denounces the priest and his steeple-house. Many of her hearers are appalled; some weep; and others listen with a rapt attention, as if a living truth had now, for the first time, forced its way through the crust of habit, reached their hearts, and awakened them to life. This matter must be looked to; else we have brought our faith across the seas with us in vain; and it had been better that the old forest were still standing here, waving its tangled boughs and murmuring to the sky out of its desolate recesses, instead of this goodly street, if such blasphemies be spoken in it.

So thought the old Puritans. What was their mode of action may be partly judged from the spectacles which now pass before your eyes. Joshua Buffum is standing in the pillory. Cassandra Southwick is led to prison. And there a woman, it is Ann Coleman,—naked from the waist upward, and bound to the tail of a cart, is dragged through the Main Street at the pace of a brisk walk, while the constable follows with a whip of knotted cords. A strong-armed fellow is that constable; and each time that he flourishes his lash in the air, you see a frown wrinkling and twisting his brow, and, at the same instant, a smile upon his lips. He loves his business, faithful officer that he is, and puts his soul into every stroke, zealous to fulfil the injunction of Major Hawthorne's warrant, in the spirit and to the letter. There came down a stroke that has drawn blood! Ten such stripes are to be given in Salem, ten in Boston, and ten in Dedham; and, with those thirty stripes of blood upon her, she is to be driven into the forest. The crimson trail goes wavering along the Main Street; but Heaven grant that, as the rain of so many years has wept upon it, time after time, and washed it all away, so there may have been a dew of mercy, to cleanse this cruel blood-stain out of the record of the persecutor's life!

Pass on, thou spectral constable, and betake thee to thine own place of torment. Meanwhile, by the silent operation of the mechanism behind the scenes, a considerable space of time would seem to have lapsed over the street. The older dwellings now begin to look weather-beaten, through the effect of the many eastern storms that have moistened their unpainted shingles and clapboards, for not less than forty years. Such is the age we would assign to the town, judging by the aspect of John Massey, the first town-born child, whom his neighbors now call Goodman Massey, and whom we see yonder, a grave, almost autumnal-looking man, with children of his own about him. To the patriarchs of the settlement, no doubt, the Main Street is still but an affair of yesterday, hardly more antique, even if destined to be more permanent, than a path shovelled through the snow. But to the middle-aged and elderly men who came hither in childhood or early youth, it presents the aspect of a long and well-established work, on which they have expended the strength and ardor of their life. And the younger people, native to the street, whose earliest recollections are of creeping over the paternal threshold, and rolling on the grassy margin of the track, look at it as one of the perdurable things of our mortal state,—as old as the hills of the great pasture, or the headland at the harbor's mouth. Their fathers and grandsires tell them how, within a few years past, the forest stood here, with but a lonely track beneath its tangled shade. Vain legend! They cannot make it true and real to their conceptions. With them, moreover, the Main Street is a street indeed, worthy to hold its way with the thronged and stately avenues of cities beyond the sea. The old Puritans tell them of the crowds that hurry along Cheapside and Fleet Street and the Strand, and of the rush of tumultuous life at Temple Bar. They describe London Bridge, itself a street, with a row of houses on each side. They speak of the vast structure of the Tower, and the solemn grandeur of Westminster Abbey. The children listen, and still inquire if the streets of London are longer and broader than the one before their father's door; if the Tower is bigger than the jail in Prison Lane; if the old Abbey will hold a larger congregation than our meeting-house. Nothing impresses them, except their own experience.

It seems all a fable, too, that wolves have ever prowled here; and not less so, that the Squaw Sachem, and the Sagamore her son, once ruled over this region, and treated as sovereign potentates with the English settlers, then so few and storm-beaten, now so powerful. There stand some school-boys, you observe, in a little group around a drunken Indian, himself a prince of the Squaw Sachem's lineage. He brought hither some beaver-skins for sale, and has already swallowed the larger portion of their price, in deadly draughts of firewater. Is there not a touch of pathos in that picture? and does it not go far towards telling the whole story of the vast growth and prosperity of one race, and the fated decay of another?—the children of the stranger making game of the great Squaw Sachem's grandson!

But the whole race of red men have not vanished with that wild princess and her posterity. This march of soldiers along the street betokens the breaking out of King Philip's war; and these young men, the flower of Essex, are on their way to defend the villages on the Connecticut; where, at Bloody Brook, a terrible blow shall be smitten, and hardly one of that gallant band be left alive. And there, at that stately mansion, with its three peaks in front, and its two little peaked towers, one on either side of the door, we see brave Captain Gardner issuing forth, clad in his embroidered buff-coat, and his plumed cap upon his head. His trusty sword, in its steel scabbard, strikes clanking on the doorstep. See how the people throng to their doors and windows, as the cavalier rides past, reining his mettled steed so gallantly, and looking so like the very soul and emblem of martial achievement,—destined, too, to meet a warrior's fate, at the desperate assault on the fortress of the Narragansetts!

"The mettled steed looks like a pig," interrupts the critic, "and Captain Gardner himself like the Devil, though a very tame one, and on a most diminutive scale."

"Sir, sir!" cries the persecuted showman, losing all patience,—for, indeed, he had particularly prided himself on these figures of Captain Gardner and his horse,—"I see that there is no hope of pleasing you. Pray, sir, do me the favor to take back your money, and withdraw!"

"Not I!" answers the unconscionable critic. "I am just beginning to get interested in the matter. Come! turn your crank, and grind out a few more of these fooleries!"

The showman rubs his brow impulsively, whisks the little rod with which he points out the notabilities of the scene, but, finally, with the inevitable acquiescence of all public servants, resumes his composure and goes on.

Pass onward, onward, Time! Build up new houses here, and tear down thy works of yesterday, that have already the rusty moss upon them! Summon forth the minister to the abode of the young maiden, and bid him unite her to the joyful bridegroom! Let the youthful parents carry their first-born to the meeting-house, to receive the baptismal rite! Knock at the door, whence the sable line of the funeral is next to issue! Provide other successive generations of men, to trade, talk, quarrel, or walk in friendly intercourse along the street, as their fathers did before them! Do all thy daily and accustomed business, Father Time, in this thoroughfare, which thy footsteps, for so many years, have now made dusty! But here, at last, thou leadest along a procession which, once witnessed, shall appear no more, and be remembered only as a hideous dream of thine, or a frenzy of thy old brain.

"Turn your crank, I say," bellows the remorseless critic, "and grind it out, whatever it be, without further preface!"

The showman deems it best to comply.

Then, here comes the worshipful Captain Curwen, sheriff of Essex, on horseback, at the head of an armed guard, escorting a company of condemned prisoners from the jail to their place of execution on Gallows Hill. The witches! There is no mistaking them! The witches! As they approach up Prison Lane, and turn into the Main Street, let us watch their faces, as if we made a part of the pale crowd that presses so eagerly about them, yet shrinks back with such shuddering dread, leaving an open passage betwixt a dense throng on either side. Listen to what the people say.

There is old George Jacobs, known hereabouts, these sixty years, as a man whom we thought upright in all his way of life, quiet, blameless, a good husband before his pious wife was summoned from the evil to come, and a good father to the children whom she left him. Ah! but when that blessed woman went to heaven, George Jacobs's heart was empty, his hearth lonely, his life broken tip; his children were married, and betook themselves to habitations of their own; and Satan, in his wanderings up and down, beheld this forlorn old man, to whom life was a sameness and a weariness, and found the way to tempt him. So the miserable sinner was prevailed with to mount into the air, and career among the clouds; and he is proved to have been present at a witch-meeting as far off as Falmouth, on the very same night that his next neighbors saw him, with his rheumatic stoop, going in at his own door. There is John Willard, too; an honest man we thought him, and so shrewd and active in his business, so practical, so intent on every-day affairs, so constant at his little place of trade, where he bartered English goods for Indian corn and all kinds of country produce! How could such a man find time, or what could put it into his mind, to leave his proper calling, and become a wizard? It is a mystery, unless the Black Man tempted him with great heaps of gold. See that aged couple,—a sad sight, truly,—John Proctor, and his wife Elizabeth. If there were two old people in all the county of Essex who seemed to have led a true Christian life, and to be treading hopefully the little remnant of their earthly path, it was this very pair. Yet have we heard it sworn, to the satisfaction of the worshipful Chief-Justice Sewell, and all the court and jury, that Proctor and his wife have shown their withered faces at children's bedsides, mocking, making mouths, and affrighting the poor little innocents in the night-time. They, or their spectral appearances, have stuck pins into the Afflicted Ones, and thrown them into deadly fainting-fits with a touch, or but a look. And, while we supposed the old man to be reading the Bible to his old wife,—she meanwhile knitting in the chimney-corner,—the pair of hoary reprobates have whisked up the chimney, both on one broomstick, and flown away to a witch-communion, far into the depths of the chill, dark forest. How foolish! Were it only for fear of rheumatic pains in their old bones, they had better have stayed at home. But away they went; and the laughter of their decayed, cackling voices has been heard at midnight, aloft in the air. Now, in the sunny noontide, as they go tottering to the gallows, it is the Devil's turn to laugh.

Behind these two,—who help another along, and seem to be comforting and encouraging each other, in a manner truly pitiful, if it were not a sin to pity the old witch and wizard,—behind them comes a woman, with a dark proud face that has been beautiful, and a figure that is still majestic. Do you know her? It is Martha Carrier, whom the Devil found in a humble cottage, and looked into her discontented heart, and saw pride there, and tempted her with his promise that she should be Queen of Hell. And now, with that lofty demeanor, she is passing to her kingdom, and, by her unquenchable pride, transforms this escort of shame into a triumphal procession, that shall attend her to the gates of her infernal palace, and seat her upon the fiery throne. Within this hour, she shall assume her royal dignity.

Last of the miserable train comes a man clad in black, of small stature and a dark complexion, with a clerical band about his neck. Many a time, in the years gone by, that face has been uplifted heavenward from the pulpit of the East Meeting-House, when the Rev. Mr. Burroughs seemed to worship God. What!—he? The holy man!—the learned!—the wise! How has the Devil tempted him? His fellow-criminals, for the most part, are obtuse, uncultivated creatures, some of them scarcely half-witted by nature, and others greatly decayed in their intellects through age. They were an easy prey for the destroyer. Not so with this George Burroughs, as we judge by the inward light which glows through his dark countenance, and, we might almost say, glorifies his figure, in spite of the soil and haggardness of long imprisonment,—in spite of the heavy shadow that must fall on him, while death is walking by his side. What bribe could Satan offer, rich enough to tempt and overcome this mail? Alas! it may have been in the very strength of his high and searching intellect, that the Tempter found the weakness which betrayed him. He yearned for knowledge he went groping onward into a world of mystery; at first, as the witnesses have sworn, he summoned up the ghosts of his two dead wives, and talked with them of matters beyond the grave; and, when their responses failed to satisfy the intense and sinful craving of his spirit, he called on Satan, and was heard. Yet—to look at him—who, that had not known the proof, could believe him guilty? Who would not say, while we see him offering comfort to the weak and aged partners of his horrible crime,—while we hear his ejaculations of prayer, that seem to bubble up out of the depths of his heart, and fly heavenward, unawares,—while we behold a radiance brightening on his features as from the other world, which is but a few steps off,—who would not say, that, over the dusty track of the Main Street, a Christian saint is now going to a martyr's death? May not the Arch-Fiend have been too subtle for the court and jury, and betrayed them—laughing in his sleeve, the while—into the awful error of pouring out sanctified blood as an acceptable sacrifice upon God's altar? Ah! no; for listen to wise Cotton Mather, who, as he sits there on his horse, speaks comfortably to the perplexed multitude, and tells them that all has been religiously and justly done, and that Satan's power shall this day receive its death-blow in New England.

Heaven grant it be so!—the great scholar must be right; so lead the poor creatures to their death! Do you see that group of children and half-grown girls, and, among them, an old, hag-like Indian woman, Tituba by me? Those are the Afflicted Ones. Behold, at this very instant, a proof of Satan's power and malice! Mercy Parris, the minister's daughter, has been smitten by a flash of Martha Carrier's eye, and falls down in the street, writhing with horrible spasms and foaming at the mouth, like the possessed one spoken of in Scripture. Hurry on the accursed witches to the gallows, ere they do more mischief!—ere they fling out their withered aims, and scatter pestilence by handfuls among the crowd!—ere, as their parting legacy, they cast a blight over the land, so that henceforth it may bear no fruit nor blade of grass, and be fit for nothing but a sepulchre for their unhallowed carcasses! So, on they go; and old George Jacobs has stumbled, by reason of his infirmity; but Goodman Proctor and his wife lean on one another, and walk at a reasonably steady pace, considering their age. Mr. Burroughs seems to administer counsel to Martha Carrier, whose face and mien, methinks, are milder and humbler than they were. Among the multitude, meanwhile, there is horror, fear, and distrust; and friend looks askance at friend, and the husband at his wife, and the wife at him, and even the mother at her little child; as if, in every creature that God has made, they suspected a witch, or dreaded an accuser. Never, never again, whether in this or any other shape, may Universal Madness riot in the Main Street!

I perceive in your eyes, my indulgent spectators, the criticism which you are too kind to utter. These scenes, you think, are all too sombre. So, indeed, they are; but the blame must rest on the sombre spirit of our forefathers, who wove their web of life with hardly a single thread of rose-color or gold, and not on me, who have a tropic-love of sunshine, and would gladly gild all the world with it, if I knew where to find so much. That you may believe me, I will exhibit one of the only class of scenes, so far as my investigation has taught me, in which our ancestors were wont to steep their tough old hearts in wine and strong drink, and indulge an outbreak of grisly jollity.

Here it comes, out of the same house whence we saw brave Captain Gardner go forth to the wars. What! A coffin, borne on men's shoulders, and six aged gentlemen as pall-bearers, and a long train of mourners, with black gloves and black hat-bands, and everything black, save a white handkerchief in each mourner's hand, to wipe away his tears withal. Now, my kind patrons, you are angry with me. You were bidden to a bridal-dance, and find yourselves walking in a funeral procession. Even so; but look back through all the social customs of New England, in the first century of her existence, and read all her traits of character; and if you find one occasion, other than a funeral feast, where jollity was sanctioned by universal practice, I will set fire to my puppet-show without another word. These are the obsequies of old Governor Bradstreet, the patriarch and survivor of the first settlers, who, having intermarried with the Widow Gardner, is now resting from his labors, at the great age of ninety-four. The white-bearded corpse, which was his spirit's earthly garniture, now lies beneath yonder coffin-lid. Many a cask of ale and cider is on tap, and many a draught of spiced wine and aqua-vitae has been quaffed. Else why should the bearers stagger, as they tremulously uphold the coffin?—and the aged pall-bearers, too, as they strive to walk solemnly beside it?—and wherefore do the mourners tread on one another's heels?—and why, if we may ask without offence, should the nose of the Rev. Mr. Noyes, through which he has just been delivering the funeral discourse, glow like a ruddy coal of fire? Well, well, old friends! Pass on, with your burden of mortality, And lay it in the tomb with jolly hearts. People should be permitted to enjoy themselves in their own fashion; every man to his taste; but New England must have been a dismal abode for the man of pleasure, when the only boon-companion was Death!

Under cover of a mist that has settled over the scene, a few years flit by, and escape our notice. As the atmosphere becomes transparent, we perceive a decrepit grandsire, hobbling along the street. Do you recognize him? We saw him, first, as the baby in Goodwife Massey's arms, when the primeval trees were flinging their shadow over Roger Conant's cabin; we have seen him, as the boy, the youth, the man, bearing his humble part in all the successive scenes, and forming the index-figure whereby to note the age of his coeval town. And here he is, old Goodman Massey, taking his last walk,—often pausing,—often leaning over his staff,—and calling to mind whose dwelling stood at such and such a spot, and whose field or garden occupied the site of those more recent houses. He can render a reason for all the bends and deviations of the thoroughfare, which, in its flexible and plastic infancy, was made to swerve aside from a straight line, in order to visit every settler's door. The Main Street is still youthful; the coeval man is in his latest age. Soon he will be gone, a patriarch of fourscore, yet shall retain a sort of infantine life in our local history, as the first town-born child.

Behold here a change, wrought in the twinkling of an eye, like an incident in a tale of magic, even while your observation has been fixed upon the scene. The Main Street has vanished out of sight. In its stead appears a wintry waste of snow, with the sun just peeping over it, cold and bright, and tingeing the white expanse with the faintest and most ethereal rose-color. This is the Great Snow of 1717, famous for the mountain-drifts in which it buried the whole country. It would seem as if the street, the growth of which we have noted so attentively, following it from its first phase, as an Indian track, until it reached the dignity of sidewalks, were all at once obliterated, and resolved into a drearier pathlessness than when the forest covered it. The gigantic swells and billows of the snow have swept over each man's metes and bounds, and annihilated all the visible distinctions of human property. So that now the traces of former times and hitherto accomplished deeds being done away, mankind should be at liberty to enter on new paths, and guide themselves by other laws than heretofore; if, indeed, the race be not extinct, and it be worth our while to go on with the march of life, over the cold and desolate expanse that lies before us. It may be, however, that matters are not so desperate as they appear. That vast icicle, glittering so cheerlessly in the sunshine, must be the spire of the meeting-house, incrusted with frozen sleet. Those great heaps, too, which we mistook for drifts, are houses, buried up to their eaves, and with their peaked roofs rounded by the depth of snow upon them. There, now, comes a gush of smoke from what I judge to be the chimney of the Ship Tavern;—and another—another—and another—from the chimneys of other dwellings, where fireside comfort, domestic peace, the sports of children, and the quietude of age are living yet, in spite of the frozen crust above them.

But it is time to change the scene. Its dreary monotony shall not test your fortitude like one of our actual New England winters, which leaves so large a blank—so melancholy a death-spot-in lives so brief that they ought to be all summer-time. Here, at least, I may claim to be ruler of the seasons. One turn of the crank shall melt away the snow from the Main Street, and show the trees in their full foliage, the rose-bushes in bloom, and a border of green grass along the sidewalk. There! But what! How! The scene will not move. A wire is broken. The street continues buried beneath the snow, and the fate of Herculaneum and Pompeii has its parallel in this catastrophe.

Alas! my kind and gentle audience, you know not the extent of your misfortune. The scenes to come were far better than the past. The street itself would have been more worthy of pictorial exhibition; the deeds of its inhabitants not less so. And how would your interest have deepened, as, passing out of the cold shadow of antiquity, in my long and weary course, I should arrive within the limits of man's memory, and, leading you at last into the sunshine of the present, should give a reflex of the very life that is flitting past us! Your own beauty, my fair townswomen, would have beamed upon you, out of my scene. Not a gentleman that walks the street but should have beheld his own face and figure, his gait, the peculiar swing of his arm, and the coat that he put on yesterday. Then, too,—and it is what I chiefly regret,—I had expended a vast deal of light and brilliancy on a representation of the street in its whole length, from Buffum's Corner downward, on the night of the grand illumination for General Taylor's triumph. Lastly, I should have given the crank one other turn, and have brought out the future, showing you who shall walk the Main Street to-morrow, and, perchance, whose funeral shall pass through it!

But these, like most other human purposes, lie unaccomplished; and I have only further to say, that any lady or gentlemen who may feel dissatisfied with the evening's entertainment shall receive back the admission fee at the door.

"Then give me mine," cries the critic, stretching out his palm. "I said that your exhibition would prove a humbug, and so it has turned out. So, hand over my quarter!"